MY AMERICAN JOU

From Log Cabin
to White House

with Abraham Lincoln

BY DEBORAH HEDSTROM-PAGE

ILLUSTRATIONS BY SERGIO MARTINEZ

FROM LOG CABIN TO WHITE HOUSE WITH ABRAHAM LINCOLN

© 2007 by B&H Publishing Group

Illustrations © 1997 by Sergio Martinez

All rights reserved.

Printed in Singapore

ISBN: 978-0-8054-3269-5

Published by B&H Publishing Group

Nashville, Tennessee

Dewey Decimal Number: F

Subject Heading: LINCOLN, ABRAHAM \ UNITED STATES HISTORY—1783-1865—FICTION \
UNITED STATES—HISTORY—1861-1865, CIVIL WAR—FICTION

Unless otherwise stated, all Scripture is taken from the HCSB, Holman Christian Standard Bible™,
copyright 1999, 2000, 2002, 2003 Holman Bible Publishers.

1 2 3 4 5 6 7 8 9 10   11 10 09 08 07

Foreword

He floated the Mississippi River, told jokes, wrestled for fun, and rarely made it to a school. But we celebrate his birthday every February, and his face appears on every penny and five-dollar bill. Many of us have even memorized his Gettysburg Address. Remember? "Four score and seven years ago, our fathers brought forth on this continent a new nation. . . ."

Abraham Lincoln was the sixteenth president of the United States, and he was one of the best known and most loved leaders of our country. He took us through the darkest period of our nation's history, when brothers fought brothers and fathers fought sons. The Civil War almost tore our country in two, but President Lincoln helped hold it together.

In this book, *From Log Cabin to White House,* you'll discover how a backwoods boy became president. You'll see him write with a burned stick, hear him split wood, feel the spray of his oars on the river, and laugh at his jokes. You'll also see him cry and pray.

As with all My American Journey books, *From Log Cabin to White House* uses a fictional character to help uncover details of America's history. This time the fictional character is Anne Hampton, a thirteen-year-old girl who lives on East Capitol Street in Washington, D.C. Anne attends Mrs. Howard's Female Academy and visits places that truly existed in 1856, when our story begins. We know they existed because they were mentioned by Frank French, a boy who grew up in Washington, D.C., and kept a diary from 1850 to 1852, starting when he was twelve years old. (If you watch carefully, near the end of the book you may find a clue asking you to imagine how well Frank and Anne knew each other.)

Like this real boy who lived 150 years ago— and probably like you—our fictional character, Anne, goes to school. Sometimes she even gets in trouble there. So like Anne, be prepared to shove aside the butterflies in your stomach and get set to open the door to a new My American Journey adventure!

Introduction

Mrs. Howard's Female Academy—Washington, D.C.
September 1856

Anne walked toward the headmistress's office, taking small steps. The longer it took to get to her doom, the better! *I can't believe I'm getting in trouble,* she thought. *The speaker didn't even look like that silly picture.*

The drawing had gone around the lecture hall while she and the other girls at the academy were waiting to hear a guest speaker discuss "The Progress of Women." They'd all groaned at the thought of listening to another spinster. That's when someone had drawn the picture of a fat lady in a black dress with pulled-back hair who looked remarkably like their last droning lecturer. The picture had circulated as today's speaker—a poised and pretty woman—began her talk. When the picture came to Anne she giggled behind her hands, trying not to be heard. But it must not have worked, because here she was, on her way to the headmistress's office. As soon as the speaker finished her talk, she'd been told to go "at once."

Even though she took small steps, Anne soon reached Mrs. Howard's office. After knocking, she heard a voice call, "Come in!" Taking a deep breath, she squeezed the wire hoop beneath her skirt so she could slip through the doorway—and then stopped in surprise.

With the headmistress was Sarah Josepha Hale, the speaker who had surprised everyone with her high-fashion ruffled silk dress and her soft brown curls. Introduced as the editor of *Godey's Lady's Book*, Mrs. Hale had held all of them spellbound in the lecture hall. She'd spoken of exercise, medical training, and the wearing of fashions that enhanced the female figure instead of dresses that simply followed the latest style. To thirteen-year-old Anne, who liked clothes but struggled with the inactivity of being ladylike, Mrs. Hale's words had been as sweet as strawberries on top of pound cake.

But now, standing in the office, Anne felt panicky. *Surely I won't be reprimanded in front of a guest.*

The headmistress said, "I've called you here because I believe your father and brothers are members of the new Republican Party."

Anne nodded but thought, *Republican Party? What about the silly picture?*

As if in answer to her confusion, Mrs. Hale explained. "Besides editing *Godey's Lady's Book*, I am determined to seek the improvement of our country and of women. This means I not only write for the magazine, urging progress, but I also write letters to our political leaders, asking for their support."

The passion behind Mrs. Hale's voice made Anne remember some of the articles she'd read in her mother's copies of *Godey's*. They had spoken of preserving President George Washington's home, building a monument on Bunker Hill, and even making Thanksgiving a national holiday.

Anne shoved these thoughts aside to listen as the editor continued. "To gain support, I must know about the politicians to whom I write," she said. "So this summer I kept track of the Republican convention held in Philadelphia and learned that a new man was gaining national popularity. Have you heard of Abraham Lincoln?"

By now Anne realized she wasn't in trouble. She was even starting to think she might be invited to work for this incredible lady. So she took a moment to think of things she'd heard before answering. "Yes, my father was impressed with the man. After returning from the convention, he said that Mr. Lincoln was honest, a good speaker, and an up-and-comer in the party."

"That is my conclusion also, and I need someone to find out about this man's past, his politics, and his progress," Mrs. Hale said. "That is why I asked your headmistress to recommend a young lady who lived in Washington, D.C., and had Republican relatives and a good pen hand." Looking directly at Anne, she added, "Mrs. Howard suggested you."

Near to bursting with excitement, Anne thought, *I'll be a correspondent just like the one Mrs. Hale hired to report on Queen Victoria in England!* Then another voice inside her head warned, *Not if you act like a giddy child, you won't!*

Immediately Anne folded her hands and tried to appear proper. She looked at Mrs. Hale and said, "I would be delighted to work for you."

After learning more of her duties, getting Mrs. Hale's address, and saying good-bye, Anne rushed to tell her friends the incredible news. This time as she headed down the hall she forgot all about taking small steps. There would be no black dress or tight bun for her—she was going to be a political correspondent for the most popular women's magazine in America!

Chapter One
BAREFOOT BEGINNINGS

Washington, D.C., October 4, 1856

Dear Mrs. Hale,

I take pen in hand to write you because I have learned much about Abraham Lincoln's past. It started when I overheard my brothers telling about Mr. Lincoln splitting logs. Later I mentioned it to my father. That set him to talking!

At first he went on and on about how most young people in 1856 don't know the kind of grit it took to build our country. He told me, "Fifty years ago 'most everybody in this town lived in cabins. Splitting logs was good, honest work, and it still is."

Then Papa went on to tell me how he had cut logs for railroad ties when he was younger than I am now. "Didn't own a pair of shoes until I was ten years old," he said.

"Is that how it was for Mr. Lincoln?" I asked him.

"Pretty near," he said. "His family moved to Indiana when it was little more than a wilderness, and they cleared land along Little Pigeon Creek. Lincoln was swinging an ax from the time he was seven years old."

Listening to my father, I even found out that Mr. Lincoln had plowed fields in his bare feet! Papa said Abe didn't have a pencil, so he wrote some of his lessons with a burned stick. He didn't have paper, either, so he wrote on boards, shaving them off after they got too messy. When he did get some paper, his cousin, Dennis Hanks, helped Abe make blackberry-juice ink. They used a turkey buzzard's quill for a pen!

More than writing, Mr. Lincoln loves to read. Anytime folks get to talking about his past, they mention Abe's book reading. "He'd walk up to fifty miles just to get a new book," they say, and "He used to gather hickory bark for a firelight to read by."

Dennis Hanks, the cousin who helped make the ink, told others, "Abe used to lay on his

stomach by the fire and read *Arabian Nights* out loud to me and his sister, Sarah. At the end, I told him it was a 'pack of lies.' Abe answered me by saying, 'Mighty fine lies.'"

Even with all this reading and writing, I'm not finding out much about the schools he attended. I know he wrote an essay about not being cruel to animals for one teacher, but I'm pretty sure our up-and-coming politician hasn't had much formal education. His pa moved the family around a lot, and when Abe wasn't working at home, he was hired out to neighbors.

It was his stepmother, Sarah Lincoln, who encouraged Abe's training, even though she can't read or write herself. She married his pa after his mother got a fever and died when Abe was only nine years old. It must have worked out well, having Miss Sarah as his stepmother, because Abe still takes trips to see her to this day.

Losing his mother wasn't the only hard thing in young Abraham Lincoln's life. Twice he almost died himself—once when he was hit in the head by a horse and once when he almost drowned after falling off a log into a creek. In spite of all this, there are lots of good tales about his growing-up years. I guess he was forever pulling pranks or telling stories. One man said, "Abe was always getting up on a stump or a box to make speeches. One day we'd laugh until our bellies hurt, and the next day he'd have us crying with his sad tales."

When I finally saw Mr. Lincoln a few nights ago after a Republican meeting, all I had heard about him made sense. Somehow his poor past and his popularity all blend together to make him seem like a very kind and caring man. He's tall and lean and doesn't give much attention to his clothes. His face looks like it was chiseled out of one of the logs he's split. Yet somehow he seems so real.

It's hard to explain. It's as if Mr. Lincoln doesn't pretend to be something he's not, like some people do. He doesn't put on airs or act all proper and dignified. And when he smiles or gets to talking and joking in his slow, country drawl, others gather around him.

But at my academy and elsewhere around the city, some speak of his poor training and ignorance of national issues. This has made me determined to find out more about his life.

I hope this letter finds you in good health and that my information proves valuable to your causes.

Cordially,

Anne Hampton

Chapter Two
FLATBOAT ADVENTURE

Washington, D.C., December 1, 1856

Dear Mrs. Hale,

From wrestling to riverboating, Mr. Lincoln had a lot of adventures after he moved away from his family! I would never have guessed that the tall, sincere man I met after the Republican meeting had lived such a life. But I learned of it from my brothers.

One night while they were playing backgammon, my brothers spoke of what it would be like to float down the Mississippi River on a flatboat. I was trying to read Shakespeare's *Hamlet*, but since it was hard going, I found myself listening to their talk instead. That's when I heard one of them say, "Abe did it."

As it turned out, a flatboat is why Lincoln left home. He'd just built one when two men asked him to row them out to a riverboat. He did so and was amazed when they flipped him two silver half-dollars. My brother quoted Lincoln as saying,

"I could scarcely believe that I, a poor boy, had earned a dollar in less than a day by honest work. It made the world seem wider and fairer before me."

Later Lincoln and another of his Hanks cousins took his flatboat down to New Orleans to sell farm produce. Traveling down the Ohio and Mississippi Rivers, they went twelve hundred miles. Once a gang of river thieves attacked them. Fists flying and oars splashing, they escaped.

Another time they watched chained slaves forced onto an auction block to be sold to the highest bidder. Lincoln speaks of it these days when he argues against the Kansas-Nebraska Act and the spreading of slavery into new territories.

This river trip and the discovery that he could earn money eventually led Lincoln to say good-bye to his pa, stepmother, and sister, who had by this time resettled in Illinois. Abe went north and found work in an Illinois river boomtown called

New Salem. He held two jobs, tending a store and logging for a mill.

My oldest brother told me what made Lincoln a town favorite. "Abe's strength in whacking down trees," he said, "led to a public wrestling match with the town champion, Jack Armstrong."

I didn't understand all my brother said about holds, takedowns, and being pinned, but I figured out that Lincoln and Armstrong wrestled to a tie.

"Abe and Jack became fast friends after their bout," my brother continued. "Their match also made the townspeople notice Lincoln."

As I listened to my brothers, I found out some other incredible things. First off, Lincoln's honesty became the talk of the town when he accidentally overcharged a customer by a few pennies and walked miles to return the man's money. Then he asked the local schoolmaster to teach him grammar and proper speech. Soon his tall tales were accompanied by speeches for river improvements. That's when folks started saying, "Abe's a thinker, and he's got a gift for speaking. He should go into politics."

But as it turned out, Abraham went to war instead.

An Indian chief named Black Hawk led his tribe across the Mississippi River, putting the Illinois settlers into a panic. The state militia was called out, and Lincoln joined. Though elected captain, he ended up fighting only mosquitoes, not Indians. Even so he kept his humor.

A friend of mine from the Rittenhouse Boys Academy told me, "Mr. Lincoln served under a colonel who was only four feet, three inches tall. At more than six feet even when slouching, Lincoln dwarfed the man. Still, the colonel corrected Abe for his poor posture. 'Hold your head high, fellow,' he told him.

"Lincoln straightened but not enough for the colonel, who commanded, 'Higher, fellow, higher!'

"Stretching up and extending his neck, Lincoln asked, 'Am I to remain this way always?'

"'Most certainly,' the colonel answered.

"In response, Lincoln got a sad look on his face and said, 'Then good-bye, Colonel, for I shall never see you again.'" My friend laughed after telling the story but it took me a minute to realize the height joke.

When released from the militia, Lincoln followed the advice of his friends and ran for representative in the Illinois legislature. He lost, but that didn't discourage him. He took jobs as the town postmaster and as deputy surveyor. Then he ran again in the same election two years later and won a seat in the Illinois House of Representatives. One man visiting my father said, "Lincoln was only twenty-four years old when he was elected to public office. But he won because he went among the people. He helped folks with chores, pitched horseshoes, refereed wrestling matches, sat in on quilting bees, and attended dances and wolf hunts."

Elected again two years later, Lincoln made the decision to leave New Salem and move to Springfield, Illinois. I'll learn more of this place and write of it in my next letter.

Thinking about what I've discovered so far, I guess it is true that Mr. Lincoln did not have the best education and training. I've heard many folks say, "It's amazing the man has gotten as far as he has in politics."

With his simple ways and unassuming airs, I do not know if he can go much further.

Most respectfully,
Anne Hampton

Chapter Three
JUDGE AND JOKESTER

Washington, D.C., March 11, 1857

Dear Mrs. Hale,

In an effort to answer your question about how Mr. Lincoln got so popular, I have found every excuse to walk past the Capitol building when Congress ends for the day. I only live a few blocks away on East Capitol Street, but this still isn't an easy task. My mother tends to worry about me because fistfights have broken out between congressmen in and around the Capitol. Our neighbor says it's because of "them gol-darned Southern politicians always causing a ruckus."

But I heard a representative from Georgia say, "Things would simmer down around here if the Northerners would stop trying to tell us what to do."

In spite of the trouble, Mother has agreed a few times to let me walk along Pennsylvania Avenue and listen to the politicians. I think this is because she is proud of my work for you. She even gave me her opinion as to why Abraham Lincoln has gotten so popular. "With all this trouble brewing over slavery, it certainly helped that he married a Southerner, Mary Todd. Though she's high-strung, she's taught him more manners and customs."

For a while I thought my mother's comment would be the only one I'd be able to send to you, because all the talk I heard on the avenue centered on slavery and the fighting it was causing in Kansas. But one day I happened upon a congressman telling another man about Lincoln becoming a lawyer.

He said, "Abe told me he almost became a blacksmith, thinking that was the most suitable work for him. But a friend by the name of John Stuart pushed Lincoln to study law. He helped him learn and even made him his law partner after Abe got his license back in '36. It proved to be a smart move, because Lincoln uses common sense and good stories in court instead of a bunch of fancy legal talk."

Walking behind the men, I also learned that Lincoln became a circuit-riding lawyer, traveling almost five hundred miles on horseback twice a year. I asked a teacher at the academy about circuit-riding lawyers. "A group of lawyers travel with a judge around his assigned circuit twice a year," she told me while circling an area on a state map with her finger. "The judge conducts trials in towns too small to have a full-time court, and the lawyers act as prosecutors and defense attorneys. Roads and bridges don't exist in many places, so they wade streams and slosh through mud. Often they must sleep on the floor of farmhouses or double up in tavern beds."

My teacher's explanation helped me understand something else I heard the congressman say. Lincoln entertained his fellow circuit riders most evenings. He'd drape his long legs over the back of a chair and tell stories. One of his favorites was about a slow horse he'd hired one time. "The nag moved like cold molasses, so when I returned it to the stable, I asked the owner if he kept the horse for funerals," Abe would say.

The owner told him no.

"Glad to hear it," Abe would say, "because if you did, the corpse wouldn't get there in time for the resurrection!"

Thinking back on this story still makes me laugh, but I need to tell you something else the congressman said since I think it explains some of Mr. Lincoln's popularity.

He said, "While Lincoln rode the circuit, he visited people, talking about crops, livestock, children, and politics. He even joined in a wrestling match or two. One lawyer who traveled with him told me that after wrestling a man who challenged him, Lincoln had to go into court with the seat of his pants ripped. The lawyer said when Abe stood up in the front of the room, you couldn't miss the tear. Finally someone sent a note around the courtroom requesting money for a pair of pants for Abe. When the note reached Lincoln, he wrote on the paper, 'I can contribute nothing to the end in view.'"

A few days later I had a chance to tell my father about what I'd heard on the avenue. He laughed at the stories I repeated but added, "Don't be fooled into thinking Abe Lincoln is nothing more than a jokester. Riding the Eighth Circuit, he's gained an excellent reputation for honesty and good sense."

One of Lincoln's law partners, William Herndon, told Papa, "Once he took the case of a Revolutionary War widow who had lost half her pension to an

agent, claiming it for his fee. Before court was over, Lincoln's passion over the injustice done to the elderly woman had half the jury in tears."

Listening to my father, I feel strongly that Abraham Lincoln's honesty must play a big part in his success. But I think his funny stories help, too, and undoubtedly my mother's comment about his wife's influence cannot be overlooked. I hope this answers your question and that you are well. Mrs. Howard's Academy will be attending a congressional session soon, and I should find out more about Lincoln's political life there.

Most sincerely,

Anne Hampton

Chapter Four
A SECOND CHANCE

Washington, D.C., October 21, 1857

Dear Mrs. Hale,

Yesterday my father took me to lunch at the Willard Hotel! It's always bustling with people from the Capitol building and the president's house. President Buchanan even walked in while I was eating some heavenly fried oysters.

Lots of people gathered around him, asking for appointments and favors. I soon feared that the luncheon would not help me discover more of Lincoln. But as my father helped me slip into my cloak, I heard a man say, "When Lincoln was here a few years back, he rivaled Ol' Henry Clay for setting off sparks in the House."

Though it wasn't much of a comment, I didn't know what to make of Lincoln having been in the Capitol before. I asked my father about it as we rode home on the omnibus. "Has Mr. Lincoln ever been elected to Congress?"

"Yes, he has," my father said over the clip-clop of horses' hooves and the rumble of carriage wheels on the cobblestones. "Represented Illinois back in the late '40s. Rented a room in a boardinghouse not far from the Capitol and lived there with his family when Congress was in session. Rubbed shoulders with politicians who went back to the early years of our country—Henry Clay, John Adams, Daniel Webster."

Hearing this, I didn't even look at the ladies' dresses as they strolled down the avenue. Instead I asked, "So why did he leave?"

"Things didn't work out," my father answered. "Abe didn't make much headway in promoting his antislavery sentiments in Congress, even though he sure stirred things up sometimes with his speeches. When then-president Polk declared war on Mexico, Lincoln was against it. He challenged President Polk to show the exact spot where American blood had been shed first. That's when Abe told Congress,

rather sarcastically, 'Young America is very anxious to fight for the liberation of enslaved nations and colonies, provided, always, that they have land.'"

Our omnibus stopped to let people on and off, but I barely noticed. "What happened? What made him return to politics?" I asked.

My father took off his top hat and ran his fingers through his hair—a sure sign that he was thinking. Finally he said, "Lincoln stayed out of politics for almost five years. Heard he went back to Illinois to practice law, and he even took time to invent a cargo lift for boats.

"But a couple of years ago the Kansas-Nebraska Act started turning those two territories into bloody battle-grounds. Settlers for and against slavery started fighting one another, hoping to get the territory made into a slave or free state. As more and more people on both sides were beaten and killed, Lincoln felt he must take a stand. He ran for Congress again in 1855, saying that slavery should not be allowed to spread and that all new territories should join the Union as free states."

"It's a good thing he was only running in Illinois," I thought aloud as we got off the omnibus. "No Southerners would have voted for him."

I'm sure I don't have to tell you, Mrs. Hale, slavery has people sizzling. You can't go any place in the capital without hearing of it, especially since the Dred Scott decision said that men of color have no rights. I hear that really upset Mr. Lincoln. While reading at the new Smithsonian Castle, I heard a man say, "Abe Lincoln pointed out that at the signing of the Declaration of Independence, free blacks were full voting citizens in five states. Now a court says they're not. Seems to me our independence is going backward."

The next day I asked my teacher why slavery was dividing the country. She told me slavery was only a side problem. "Money and states' rights are the real issues," she said. "The South needs slaves to work its cotton fields, and it needs low trading fees to ship its cotton overseas. But the North's new factories want high trading fees to keep out foreign products."

"But what of the abolitionists?" I asked.

"They speak up, but they're in the minority," she told me. "Most people don't care about slaves. Look at our city. Twenty percent of our fifty-five thousand citizens are free blacks, Anne, but while you can attend any number of public and private schools, there is only one school for Negro girls your age. And people of color don't live in homes like yours but in run-down buildings off muddy alleys."

My teacher's words made me think of sections of town that my family avoided. They were known for their shootings, stabbings, and riots. Picturing the dirty, dingy buildings, I wondered how Mr. Lincoln really felt about people of color. A while later, I got my answer in church.

The sermon had been about loving your brother, and after the service a man asked the minister how he could love a black person. "The same way that Abe Lincoln is learning to," the minister answered. "Lincoln started out like most of us, thinking Negroes were lower-class people. But seeing chain gangs, watching slave auctions, and listening to abolitionists is changing him a little every day. Leave your mind open to the truth about all people, and you'll change too."

The fretting and arguing over slavery makes my head spin. Sometimes I don't know what to write to you. But maybe Mr. Lincoln got back into politics and is becoming well-known because he has an open mind that keeps learning and growing.

With high regard,
Anne Hampton

Chapter Five
MURDER BY MOONLIGHT

Washington, D.C., December 2, 1858

Dear Mrs. Hale,

I know I haven't written for some time, but having told you all about Mr. Lincoln's past, I needed to wait until he did something of note. He has! News of the murder trial and the debates he's involved in have made it to Washington quickly, even though Lincoln is still in Illinois.

I learned of the murder while attending the play *Uncle Tom's Cabin* at Ford's Theater. At intermission, I lingered in the hall, admiring the side boxes with their satin-and-lace curtains and fancy chandeliers. That's when I overheard two ladies talking. "At the trial, tears ran down Mr. Lincoln's cheeks," the taller one said, "when he spoke of the young man's widowed mother losing her only son to a hangman's noose. My sister, who lives in Springfield and heard it, said it was most heart-wrenching."

"I have little doubt of that," the shorter woman replied, "but my John says it was a brilliant stroke on

Lincoln's part to use the almanac in defending the son. The eyewitness admitted he was 150 feet away from the fight but said the night's moonlight allowed him to clearly see the widow's son strike and kill the victim. By using the almanac, Lincoln proved that on the night of the murder the moon had already set when the murder occurred—so there wasn't nearly enough light to see from so far a distance."

I listened for the trial's outcome, but instead the women started talking about the actor playing Uncle Tom. So I left to search the lobby for my father. Finding him, I asked about the murder trial.

"Lincoln got the young man off," he told me. "From all I heard, he put on a splendid defense. And it wasn't the only case he's won. Just recently he defended the Illinois Central Railroad and got himself a five-thousand-dollar fee." Lowering his voice, he added, "Talk in the party is that Lincoln can now pay for a strong congressional campaign."

My father's words came true when the Republicans in Illinois nominated Lincoln to run against Stephen Douglas for U.S. senator. Abe's speech accepting the nomination caused a real to-do. In it he said the country was "a house divided." He told the convention, "I believe this government cannot endure, permanently, half slave and half free. It will become all one thing, or all the other."

In addition, Mr. Lincoln challenged Mr. Douglas to seven debates. Everywhere people speak of them; thousands of listeners gather to hear the two candidates in every city that hosts a debate. I even heard the Lincoln-Douglas debates mentioned at the circus a few days ago. My friends and I were clapping for a man who walked on glass bottles when a boy near us said to his pals, "Did you hear what Abe Lincoln said at the last debate? It was first rate!"

His friends shook their heads, and I listened with them as the boy told what happened. "After going on a bit, Douglas called Lincoln two-faced. Later, when it was Abe's turn to speak, he mentioned the insult and said, 'I leave it to my audience. If I had another face, do you think I would wear this one?'"

The debates are also in the newspapers regularly. I picked up one that said Douglas spoke with a commanding voice and impressive gestures while Lincoln had a gawky figure and made absurd up-and-down movements for emphasis. In spite of this, the journalist ended by writing, "Yet the open-minded person felt at once that, while on one side a skillful debater argued for a wrong and weak cause, there was on the other side a thoroughly earnest and truthful man defending sound convictions."

Though Lincoln spoke well and ran a good campaign, he lost the election. I found out more of this when my academy went to visit the Capitol building. We were to see the House of Representatives, but a boys' academy was already there, so we went into the Senate. This proved fortunate, because there I heard two senators talking about the election.

"After losing, Lincoln said he felt like a boy who had stubbed his toe—too big to cry and too badly hurt to laugh," one of the men said.

"Maybe so," the other senator replied, "but he'll be on the rise now, probably in a national election next time."

At first I thought I heard the man wrong. *How could losing an election help Mr. Lincoln?* I wondered.

Leaning forward in my seat, I listened carefully as the man continued, "Douglas is a top politician, yet he only won by carrying the state senate districts. More people actually voted for Lincoln, but Douglas's party won more seats in the Illinois senate, and it's the state senates that select the U.S. senators.

Believe me, the Republicans will take notice of this raw backwoodsman. They'd be fools not to."

The rest of the time in the Senate was boring until a fight broke out between a Southern congressman and a Northern senator. Mrs. Howard rushed us out, and we went back to the academy. One of my friends, who is a bit of a tomboy, grumbled as we walked. "I bet the boys academy didn't have to leave."

As she grumbled, I looked at the "stump." It's the half-finished pillar started a long time ago to honor George Washington. Then I looked back at the half-finished top of the Capitol building and its two unfinished additions. With all the North and South problems, I wonder if these huge projects will ever be finished.

The torn-up buildings. The Senate fight. They made me think of Mr. Lincoln's speech about a nation divided not being able to endure. If he ever does get elected to a big office, I sure hope he can do something to fix things.

Respectfully,
Anne Hampton

Chapter Six
HALF HORSE, HALF ALLIGATOR

Washington, D.C., November 18, 1860

Dear Mrs. Hale,

Part of Washington is cheering, and part is in a pucker. Mr. Lincoln's getting elected as president has people split down the middle. Northern newspapers are printing "Let the People Rejoice!" while Southern papers say, "Evil Days Are Upon Us!" I even heard one of my brothers say that Lincoln is getting hate mail every day.

A few months ago, I might not have believed my brother, but now I think it's true. Living in the capital, I've heard Mr. Lincoln called plenty of names, but mostly the jokesters poked fun at his tall awkwardness or his humble background. Like the man who called him "half horse and half alligator." Most of those things were just said in fun. But these days I hear him called terrible names I can't even repeat. Then at church a week ago, a member told my father, "My brother in Florida wrote that folks are hanging man-sized dolls by the neck with 'Lincoln' signs pinned to them."

But the worst thing happened when I went to get President Buchanan's autograph. He will be leaving when Mr. Lincoln takes over the presidency in two months, so Mrs. Howard said that now was our last chance to get the fifteenth president's signature.

I got the autograph, but when I was walking down the front hall of the president's house, two men burst in the door. "They're leaving the Union," one was saying, "and talking of forming the Southern confederacy."

"South Carolina's representatives have always been hotheaded," the second man replied. "It's probably just one more threat. But we'd best tell Buchanan, though I doubt he'll do much."

I didn't walk home but hurried to an omnibus. I kept wanting to tell the driver to go faster. I had to tell my father what I'd heard. He would know what

to do. But he didn't. He just shook his head and said, "It was bound to come. Tensions have been running too high for too long."

"But Father," I interrupted, "what will become of our country? Surely you can do something!"

"No, Anne," my father said as he laid a comforting hand on my shoulder. "We cannot control the actions of others, only our own. And as for our country, I fear a civil war. I do not envy Abraham Lincoln, his new presidency, nor the decisions he must make."

I went up to my room and plopped on my bed, unmindful of my hoop skirt. Sitting there, I thought back to all the excitement in our home when Mr. Lincoln gave his first big lecture and then when he got the presidential nomination and won the election.

My brothers went all the way to New York City to hear Mr. Lincoln's speech. In spite of the large crowd that attended, my older brother said, "At first I believed all was lost. On stage Lincoln looked tall and awkward. His clothes were wrinkled and didn't fit well. When he said 'Mr. *Cheerman*' instead of 'Mr. *Chairman*,' I thought, *This won't do. This might work in the country, but it will never go down in New York City!*

"But when Lincoln got warmed up, his gestures smoothed out, his face lit up with his passion, and he was transformed. I forgot his rumpled clothes,

gangly height, and unruly hair. Soon I was on my feet with everyone else, yelling like a wild Indian.

"Walking out of the hall, I saw a fellow all aquiver like myself and asked him what he thought of Lincoln the rail-splitter. He said, 'He's the greatest man since Saint Paul.'"

A few months later both my father and brothers went to the Republican convention that nominated Lincoln for president. They returned with glowing reports. "It was close. Real close. But when the winning vote was taken, thousands of us cheered wildly," my father said.

During the campaign, I proudly wore a Lincoln button on my cloak, and one of his coins dangled from my bracelet. My father and brothers spoke often on Lincoln's behalf, and our whole family could hardly sleep the night the votes were counted.

Thinking about it now, I can't understand how the thrill of learning Abraham Lincoln won the presidency could change so much. Right now I just feel afraid of war. Lying down on my bed, I confess, I had a good cry.

Sadly yours,
Anne Hampton

Chapter Seven
YANKEE AGAINST REBEL

Washington, D.C., July 2, 1862

Dear Mrs. Hale,

President Lincoln looks different these days—more chiseled and graver even when he laughs and smiles. He's taken to wearing a beard too. I've heard people say the change is due to mistakes made early in his presidency that caused lost battles. Others think it is the death of yet another of his sons. I don't know who is right, but at a neighbor's barbecue I heard Lincoln tell his friend, Mr. Seward, "I enjoyed politics immensely before becoming president. I was even eager to hold the highest office in the land. But in the president's house, instead of glory, I've found only ashes and blood."

It's not just the president's house that seems so grim. Soldiers and tales of battle fill our city. When Southern troops marched against us, Union regiments rushed to defend the capital . . . and they just kept coming. Now tents and uniforms fill all our open spaces: the Capitol grounds, the Georgetown College campus, and lots of other areas.

Thousands of wounded soldiers crowd our hospitals too. I volunteer in the one closest to my home. A clerk from the patent office, Clara Barton, is organizing the volunteers and doing a good job in maintaining supplies. Also a poet named Walt Whitman helps to tend the wounded. But even with these fine people to work beside me, sometimes I just want to go home. I am not sure if it is the work or the heartache of torn bodies and death.

Both my brothers joined the fighting, and sometimes what I see at the hospital makes me feel a cold fear for them. I pray each night that God will somehow keep them safe against cannon, rifle, and saber.

I write many letters for the wounded soldiers in the hospital, who are often terribly homesick. Like myself, they've never been far from home before. Since pen and ink are scarce, usually I can only write

their letters in pencil. But I think they'd use burned sticks and boards if it were the only way to send news home. In fact, one day at the post I saw so many letters I mentioned it to the clerk. She told me, "The war is causing folks to write like never before. Most days we handle ninety thousand letters, and the bigger post office—the one in Louisville—handles twice that many."

While the soldiers write letters, the president is becoming known for writing pardons. My father says it has riled some of the officers, and General Butler even sent Lincoln a telegram saying, "I pray you not to interfere with the courts-martial of the army. You will destroy all discipline among our soldiers."

"The very next day," my father told me, "an old man came to the president, asking for a pardon for his son. He read Butler's telegram to the old man and said he could do nothing. The man looked so sad that Abe reached for paper and wrote, 'Job Smith is not to be shot until further orders from me—A. Lincoln.'

"Still unhappy, the elder Smith said, 'But you could order him shot tomorrow.'

"Lincoln smiled at that and said, 'If your son never dies until orders come from me to shoot him, he will live to be a great deal older than Methuselah.'"

The president's humor and storytelling during these dark days anger some folks. One day while I waited to see the president about getting more quinine and brandy for the hospital, I heard a congressman yelling at Lincoln. The walls did not stop his harsh words. "That is the way with you, sir— story! story! You are the father of every military blunder that has been made during this war. You are on the road to perdition, sir."

How I wished I could have prevented the man's words! I know the president feels the weight of every battle lost and every person slain. His stand on the war and ending slavery has been attacked on every side: by abolitionists, conservatives, states' righters, and armchair generals. But how can anyone lay this war at only his feet? Besides, he told my father why he jokes. "I laugh in these dark days of war," the president said, "because I must not cry."

I do not believe that laughter always stops our president's tears, and he, too, is in my prayers along with my brothers. I believe he thinks the only thing that can justify the terrible loss of life in this war is permanent freedom for the slaves.

Faithfully,

Anne Hampton

Chapter Eight
THANKSGIVING

Washington, D.C., December 19, 1863

Dear Mrs. Hale,

Listening to my father thank the dear Lord for our many blessings on the last Thursday of last month, I felt a new hope stir within me. Mrs. Hale, you were right. During this dark time, we need to somehow be thankful. I'm glad you've kept on for all these years, writing hundreds of letters and many editorials in an effort to establish a national day of thanksgiving.

Your letter requesting the holiday must have seemed a breath of fresh air to the president after the battle at Gettysburg. Many say the South will never recover from the blow of its losses. So many men died! My own younger brother was wounded there and is now home. To this day he does not speak to me of the fighting.

It took time for news of his injury to reach us, but when it did, my father left to bring him home. After returning, Father said, "Gettysburg is not a place for the fainthearted. Even now, four months after the battle, piles of coffins still wait for burial."

He also said that while waiting for my brother's release, he heard the president speak at the dedication of the national cemetery being established there. "The main speaker went on for more than two hours," my father told us, "yet I cannot remember what he said. The president followed with a speech of only ten sentences, yet I will never forget a single word."

As his speech at Gettysburg showed, the war has deeply affected President Lincoln. He doesn't laugh as much these days, and when I saw him last, I could tell he has lost weight. Many say he does not sleep well. Yet every day he presses on. He even visited the hospital where I volunteer. Walking among the rows of beds, he stopped in amazement when he saw a soldier taller than himself whose feet hung off the cot. Grinning, he held out his

hand to the fellow and said, "Hello, comrade, do you know when your feet get cold?"

Both men shared a fine laugh, and it was good to know that the war hadn't taken away all the president's humor.

A much shorter soldier also caught the president's attention recently. Johnny Clem is only twelve years old, but a Confederate cavalry captured him in October. Immediately officials made plans for his exchange. He is a kind of national hero since newspapers printed his story about a year ago.

Johnny tried to join the Union army when he was only nine years old. Turned down, he tagged along with a Massachusetts regiment until the men made Johnny their drummer boy. He went on to survive the battles of Chickamauga and Shiloh, earning the nickname "Johnny Shiloh." Last I heard, he is to be made a general's aide, and he has changed his name to John Lincoln Clem.

For those of us working to relieve the suffering of the soldiers, there is yet another reason for gratitude. The U.S. Sanitary Commission believed it had to disband due to lack of money, but volunteers in Chicago thought of having a "Sanitary Fair" to raise funds. Five thousand people paid to tour the exhibits, eat, and attend an auction. People bought pianos, toys, clothes, flowers, and other donated items. The item that brought the most money came from President Lincoln. He donated the original draft of the Emancipation Proclamation, and it sold for three thousand dollars!

Since then our town and many others have held similar fairs. It's almost a competition to see who can put on the best auction and earn the most money. Our city did well, but both New York and Philadelphia raised a million dollars!

Walking home from the hospital, I see even more reasons to give thanks. The Capitol building is finished! Its new iron dome is tall and stately, and its added wings make it look like a palace. Now only the Washington Monument remains unfinished.

I think that someday there will also be a Lincoln Memorial. The president has done so much, including issuing the Proclamation of Amnesty and Reconstruction. It promises full pardons to all who resume allegiance to the United States.

Though this awful war is not over, my father says this offer of pardon provides a way for our country to mend and heal when the fighting finally stops.

Yes, I had much to be thankful for on America's first national Thanksgiving—especially for the Almighty giving our country a man like President Abraham Lincoln to take us through our darkest hour.

With thanks,

Anne Hampton

Epiloque
DARKNESS AND LIGHT

Washington, D.C., December 10, 1865

Dear Mrs. Hale,

Your need for information about the president is long past, and your campaign for a national Thanksgiving holiday is a success. But I wanted to write and congratulate you on the publishing of your recent book, *Sketches of Distinguished Women.*

As I read it, I could almost see you as you were years ago, speaking to my class at Mrs. Howard's Academy. Though you have long had a passion for your causes and for women's rights, you have always looked, spoken, or acted like a fine lady. I can think of no better person to write about distinguished women.

I was also happy to see that some of President Lincoln's jokes were published in a book. These days his humor and easy ways tend to get lost in the memories of his terrible death. How well I recall my own horror and tears upon learning that the president was shot while attending a play in Ford's Theater.

It seemed so senseless. The Civil War was over, and full pardons had been promised to all.

If only that awful John Booth could have realized that murdering the president would make it worse for the South, not better! Instead of President Lincoln's easy pardons, the Southerners have ended up with a program of punishment—plantations and arms have been seized, and carpetbaggers have made it rich off the South's misery. Even today, I sometimes think, *If only the president had lived.*

I do not believe I will ever forget Mr. Lincoln's last speech. It took place two days after Lee had surrendered, ending the war. Three thousand people cheered in our streets. Then Lincoln stood at a window in the president's house and spoke to the crowd about putting the country back together. From my position, I heard a man yell, "What shall we do with the Rebels?"

From among the crowd, another yelled, "Hang them!"

That's when I saw Lincoln's son, Tad, get his father's attention and speak to him. Straightening up after stooping to hear his son, Mr. Lincoln said, "That's right, Tad. We don't want to hang them. We want to hang on to them."

Shortly after that speech, I attended the president's funeral. Our entire city mourned. The hospital volunteer and poet, Walt Whitman, even wrote a poem called "O Captain! My Captain!" that echoed our sorrow.

I did not watch the entire procession accompanying the black-draped carriage. Too many tears had given me a terrible headache. Later, when I felt better, my father came and spoke to me. His words gave me comfort.

He said, "Right before Gettysburg, I went to the president's house to speak with Mr. Lincoln. He seemed more confident than he had for a long time, and I asked him why.

"He told me, 'Yesterday, I felt that we'd reached a great crisis. I went to my room, knelt down, and prayed. Never before had I prayed with so much earnestness. I felt I must put all my trust in Almighty God. He gave our people the best country ever given to man. He alone could save it from destruction.

I had tried my best to do my duty . . . and found myself unequal to the task. The burden was more than I could bear. I asked him to help us and give us victory. When I got up, I was sure my prayer was answered.'"

Remembering my father's words now, years later, I realize that God did answer President Lincoln's prayer. Neither Mr. Booth nor the vengeance-driven politicians stopped God's answer, for once again, we are the United States of America.

Sincerely,

Anne Hampton French

Responsibility

Character Building with Abraham Lincoln

Responsibility:

When Words Meet Actions

Your parents and teachers have probably said the word, but it's not a kid kind of word. It's long, and you have to get through six syllables just to say it.

"Re-spon-si-bil-i-ty." But the word's big size fits because it stands for a big idea. It's easy to say, "Sure, I'll do that." But things come up. A friend wants to do something. A good television show comes on. The computer game blinks that you're winning. A math assignment is too hard. Or you just don't feel like it.

The list of things that can sidetrack you from doing what you need to is endless. But if you're responsible, you try and do it anyway. Or to put it another way, if it's your job to make your bed and do your homework, you do it. No wonder responsibility is such a big idea. It affects all the things we do and don't do!

In the book you've just read, *From Log Cabin to White House with Abraham Lincoln*, you see a good example of a responsible person. Abraham Lincoln always had things to do, and the older he got, the harder those things became. What made him plow fields instead of play? Why did he want the added responsibility of being elected to an office? How could he do what he didn't want to do? Looking at possible answers to these questions, along with digging into Bible verses and the quotes of others, you'll begin to see why Abraham Lincoln chose to become a responsible person. It should also help you discover what God thinks about responsibility. And maybe, just maybe, it might help you do your homework and chores!

CHAPTER ONE

Barefoot Beginnings

Life has no meaning except in terms of responsibility.
REINHOLD NIEBUHR

1. Review chapter one and write down at least four things that Abraham Lincoln was supposed to do as a kid.

_____

_____

_____

_____

Don't forget that he used his ax for two different jobs on and off his parents' farm, and that he had homework even when he didn't go to school.

2. Think back to what it must have been like to live on a farm. Write down three things that you might want to do instead of plow fields.

_____

_____

_____

STUCK? Remember Abe would be close to creeks, fields, animals, and caves. Plus he had cousins he enjoyed!

W H A T   T H E   B I B L E   S A Y S

Read 1 Corinthians 3:8
Now the one who plants and the one who waters are equal,
and each will receive his own reward according to his own labor.

This verse says that no matter what job a person is responsible to do, it has purpose and brings a reward. Using the example of cleaning a room, write down a possible purpose and reward for this responsibility.

HINT: *To find the purpose of something, ask yourself,* Why is it helpful or valuable to do this?

I T ' S   Y O U R   T U R N

Make a list of the things you are expected to do during the week. Can you think of one or two reasons why each of the things on your list needs to be done?

CHAPTER   TWO

Flatboat Adventure

*The willingness to accept responsibility for one's own life
is the source from which self-respect springs.*

J O A N   D I D I O N

1. Abraham Lincoln grows up and leaves home in this chapter. Without parents to tell him what to do, do Abe's responsibilities increase or decrease?_____

2. Write down three responsibilities that Abe had after leaving home.

_____

_____

_____

Besides being responsible to his employers and his country, Abe returned to school!

2. Which do you think is harder, being responsible for what you are told to do or being responsible when it's only up to you? Why?

_____

_____

STUCK? If a teacher told a class they only needed to do homework if they felt they should, how many kids would do it? Being responsible on your own can be hard!

W H A T   T H E   B I B L E   S A Y S

Read Acts 6:1–3
In those days, as the number of the disciples was multiplying,
there arose a complaint by the Hellenistic Jews against the Hebraic Jews
that their widows were being overlooked in the daily distribution.
Then the Twelve . . . said, ". . . Select from among you seven men
of good reputation, full of the Spirit and wisdom,
whom we can appoint to this duty."

In the verses above a problem about food was splitting apart the early church. It could only be solved if some people accepted the responsibility of dividing the food equally. What would have happened if the seven men had forgotten or been too busy to be responsible?

I T ' S   Y O U R   T U R N

Make a second list of self responsibilities. (Ones that no one will hassle you about if you don't do them. Some things might be going to sports practice, feeding a hamster or bird, fixing something you broke, doing extra yard work to earn money.)

How dependable are you to do these things?

Ask God to help you do one thing that's hard for you to be responsible about.

Judge and Jokester

Responsibility educates.

WENDELL PHILLIPS

1. In chapter three, Lincoln becomes a circuit-riding lawyer. Write down three responsibilities he had after taking this job.

_____

_____

_____

Don't forget that besides traveling and defending folks in court, Lincoln had to prepare his cases.

2. Looking at the list above, it is obvious that Lincoln had a lot of responsibility, but that didn't make him fretful and serious all the time. What were two fun things that Lincoln did while being a circuit lawyer?

_____

_____

STUCK? *Besides telling jokes, what sport did Lincoln love?*

W H A T   T H E   B I B L E   S A Y S

Read 1 Chronicles 15:22
Chenaniah, the leader of the Levites in music,
was to direct the music because he was skillful.

Often the way people use the word *responsibility* makes is seem hard and awful. But this verse
in 1 Chronicles gives some positive thoughts about responsibility. Can you name one or two of them?

I T ' S   Y O U R   T U R N

Look back over your previous lists and ask God to show you something positive about them. Is there
anything you can do to make them more fun? An example might be racing your brother or sister to
see who can clean their room the fastest and best.

CHAPTER FOUR

A Second Chance

Liberty means responsibility. That is why most men dread it.
GEORGE BERNARD SHAW

1. A big part of responsibility is doing what you believe is right. In chapter four we find two things that Lincoln strongly believed. Write down what they were.

_____

_____

One had to do with slaves, the other had to do with a war.

2. Not everyone agreed with Lincoln, and he lost his seat in Congress. After this hard defeat, Lincoln tried to stay away from political responsibility. But after a while he accepted it again. Why? (Look back on page 22.)

_____

_____

3. Once elected, Mr. Lincoln didn't just sit around. How did he act on his belief?

_____

_____

STUCK? *Look back at the end of page 23.*

WHAT THE BIBLE SAYS

Read Matthew 27:24
When Pilate saw that he was getting nowhere,
but that a riot was starting instead,
he took some water, washed his hands in front of the crowd,
and said, "I am innocent of this man's blood.
See to it yourselves!"

When being responsible gets hard, most people want to quit. In the above verse, that is what Pilate did. He refused to judge Jesus. But by refusing to accept his responsibility as judge, what did he actually do to Jesus?

IT'S YOUR TURN

Sometimes we think choosing to do or not do what we are responsible for only affects us. But this is usually not the case. Pick two things from your list on page 46. If you do not do these, who else is affected?

Ask God to help you remember others when you don't want to do the above jobs.

CHAPTER FIVE

Murder by Moonlight

I believe that every right implies a responsibility.

JOHN D. ROCKEFELLER JR.

1. What life-or-death responsibility does Lincoln accept in chapter five?

_____

_____

Think of the penalty for the crime his client was accused of.

2. What work did Lincoln have to do in order to prove his client's innocence?

_____

_____

STUCK? *Who did he have to talk to? What did he have to read?*

3. After losing another big election, how did Lincoln feel?

_____

_____

STUCK? *Peek back at page 26.*

W H A T   T H E   B I B L E   S A Y S

Read Nehemiah 13:10–11
*I [Nehemiah] also found out that because the portions for the Levites
had not been given, each of the Levites and the singers
performing the service had gone back to his own field.
Therefore, I rebuked the officials, saying,
"Why has the house of God been neglected?"*

In the Old Testament, the Levites were to work in the temple, not in the fields. This meant they didn't have food unless people brought bulls and grain to sacrifice to God. When the people quit their responsibility of sacrificing, what happened?

I T ' S   Y O U R   T U R N

Write down some of the reasons why you don't always do your responsibilities.
Ask God to help you get past them, even if they seem good ones.

Half Horse, Half Alligator

Responsibility walks hand in hand with capacity and power.

J. G. H O L L A N D

1. When Abraham Lincoln accepted the responsibility of becoming president in 1861, what huge problem did he face?

_____

_____

_____

Remember that the choices Lincoln made could start or avoid a civil war.

2. Many people didn't support Lincoln as president. Write down three things that show this.

_____

_____

_____

STUCK? *Review the newspaper headlines, Lincoln's mail, and the crowds in the South.*

W H A T ' S   T H E   B I B L E   S A Y S

Read Galatians 6:4
But each person should examine his own work,
and then he will have a reason for boasting in himself alone,
and not in respect to someone else.

The above verse says that accepting responsibility is not a matter of what others say about us, but a matter of how we feel about what we've done. Besides God, who is the one person who knows if you have done your best on a job?

I T ' S   Y O U R   T U R N

Go back over your lists of responsibilities and ask yourself if you do them the best you can. Be honest. This is between you and God, and He already knows anyway!

If you are not doing your best, ask God to help you improve.

CHAPTER SEVEN

Yankee against Rebel

We say we are for the Union. The world will not forget that we say this.
We know how to save the Union. The world knows we do know how to save it.
We, even we here, hold the power and bear the responsibility.

ABRAHAM LINCOLN

1. When President Lincoln decided that the Southern states couldn't break off from the country, name three hard things that happened.

_____

_____

_____

Think about how a civil war affects a country—crops, people, jobs, health.

2. Lincoln made mistakes, and as the war continued, he found his responsibility harder and harder to bear. Write down two things that show this.

_____

_____

STUCK? *Reread the section about Lincoln's appearance and what he said.*

WHAT THE BIBLE SAYS

Read Genesis 3:12–13
Then the man replied, "The woman You gave to be with me—
she gave me some fruit from the tree, and I ate."...
And the woman said, "It was the serpent. He deceived me, and I ate."

When Adam and Eve sinned in the garden, neither accepted responsibility for what they had done. How did they try to avoid it?

IT'S YOUR TURN

Have you ever tried to excuse one of your not-done responsibilities by blaming it on someone else? Such as, "The coach kept me too late" or "But Mary didn't do hers either."

If you often try to avoid responsibility by blaming others, talk to God about it and ask Him to help you stick to comments about yourself.

Thanksgiving

The most important thought I ever had
was that of my individual responsibility to God.
DANIEL WEBSTER

1. How do you think President Lincoln felt when he saw the stacks of coffins on the battlefield at Gettysburg?

_____

_____

Remember the president had lost weight and didn't sleep well.

2. What did President Lincoln finally do when his responsibilities were too hard for him to carry? (Look in the epilogue on page 39.)

_____

_____

STUCK? *Who is the one being strong enough to carry anything?*

3. Go back to page 41 and fill in Lincoln's words:

I had tried my _____ *to do my duty and found myself*

_____ *to the task. I asked him to*_____ *us.*

W H A T   T H E   B I B L E   S A Y S

Read 1 Peter 5:6–7
Humble yourselves therefore under the mighty hand of God,
so that He may exalt you in due time,
casting all your care upon Him, because He cares about you.

Sometimes we honestly try but fail at being responsible. According to this verse, why should we give this hard area to God?

I T ' S   Y O U R   T U R N

Look again at your list of responsibilities. Tell God where you have failed and how hard it is. Don't blame others or things but just say where you blew it. Then ask Him to help you do better, day by day, little by little.

Activities

From Log Cabin to White House with Abraham Lincoln

Journalists Wanted

Young and energetic correspondents needed to cover upcoming presidential race between Abraham Lincoln and Stephen Douglas. Journalists will also report on the widening gap between the Northern and Southern states over the slavery issue. In case of a civil war, applicants must be willing to visit the front lines and field hospital and do other dangerous assignments.

NEW YORK TIMES

See if you can earn a press pass by doing the activities on the following pages. Uncover the answers to the clues given on each page and fill in the blanks correctly. There are numbers under some of the letters in your clue answer. Take those numbered letters and fill them in the appropriate spaces on the back page of this book. When all spaces are filled, you'll discover what the headlines read at the end of the Civil War. You will also earn the title of official newspaper press correspondent!

Example: Clue Answer   F o r t   S u m t e r
                                   2   7

             Back Page   o   m
                          1 2 3 4   5 6 7 8 9 10

The Campaign Trail

Presidential campaigns today are high tech. Candidates appear on TV, haveWeb sites, and take jets from state to state. But in 1860 things were different! Politicians hired professional shriekers to cheer with the crowds. At the Republican Convention in Chicago, the shriekers got so loud that one journalist said, "It sounded like all the hogs in Cincinnati were giving their death squeals."

Even after Lincoln won the nomination, he didn't know it. Without telephones, he had to wait until a telegram arrived at his home in Springfield, Illinois.

The Republican Convention in Chicago

A House Divided

When Abraham Lincoln was nominated as the Republican candidate for president, he gave a speech that became famous. He said that the nation couldn't prosper without solving the slavery issue. "A house divided against itself can't stand," he said.

What was the name of the bird that young Lincoln took quills from to make his pens? Look in the Did You Know? section and fill in the answer in the blanks below. Write the same letter above the numbered space in the space with the matching number on page 82.

___ ___ ___ ___   ___ ___   ___ ___
6   24   21   13

Lincoln-Douglas Debates

Before Lincoln won the presidency, he lost an election to the U.S. Senate. Seven times he debated his opponent, Stephen Douglas. In cities throughout Illinois, they argued for three hours about the hot issues that were tearing the country apart. Up to 15,000 people attended each of these open-air debates. Sometimes they listened in blazing sun, once in light rain. Newspapers across the nation carried their arguments. Though Lincoln lost the election, he gained a national reputation as a rising star in the new Republican Party.

Campaign Promotions

Campaign buttons decorated the wool coats and cotton blouses of many Americans. Popular Lincoln campaign coins also dangled from bracelets and pocket watch chains, called "fobs."

Republican Ticket

Until the Republican Party picked his vice president, Abraham Lincoln had never met his running mate, Senator Hannibal Hamlin from Maine. This seems strange now, but remember, a trip from Illinois to Maine would take days by horse and buggy or railroad.

CHARLESTON MERCURY

EXTRA:

Passed unanimously at 1.15 o'clock, P. M., December 20th, 1860.

AN ORDINANCE

To dissolve the Union between the State of South Carolina and other States united with her under the compact entitled "The Constitution of the United States of America."

We, the People of the State of South Carolina, in Convention assembled, do declare and ordain, and it is hereby declared and ordained,

That the Ordinance adopted by us in Convention, on the twenty-third day of May, in the year of our Lord one thousand seven hundred and eighty-eight, whereby the Constitution of the United States of America was ratified, and also, all Acts and parts of Acts of the General Assembly of this State, ratifying amendments of the said Constitution, are hereby repealed; and that the union now subsisting between South Carolina and other States, under the name of "The United States of America," is hereby dissolved.

THE UNION IS DISSOLVED!

Newspaper Headlines

Tension between the North and South made Abraham Lincoln's election as president the final reason to start the Civil War. While Northerners cheered the victory of an antislavery candidate, Southerners felt outraged and started voting state by state to leave the Union.

Washington, D.C.

Washington, D.C., in 1860, looked a lot different from the United States capital today. Instead of thousands of buses and cars zipping down four-lane paved streets, horse-drawn buggies and omnibuses rolled over cobblestones. And instead of stately monuments and lush green lawns surrounding our government buildings, half-finished building projects and open fields set them off.

The Smithsonian Institution

Today this red castle houses fourteen separate museums and galleries, as well as the National Zoo and libraries containing 1.2 million books. Called the "Nation's Attic," it has national treasures such as the airplane the Wright brothers flew and the original Star-Spangled Banner.

White House

Every U.S. president except George Washington has lived at 1600 Pennsylvania Avenue. After eight years of building, the White House was finished in 1800 and contained 62 rooms. Fifty years ago it was remodeled and now has 132 rooms! Since first becoming the home of our presidents, it's had many names. Though called the White House today, it's also been called the President's Palace, President's House, and Executive Mansion. The president's family lives on the second floor. The third floor contains guest rooms and staff quarters.

Omnibus

Networks of omnibuses provided public transportation in Washington, D.C., and many other cities in the 1860s. These early buses looked a lot like San Francisco's famous cable cars but they were pulled by teams of horses or mules. The driver stopped and let passengers off when one tugged on the rope that was tied around his ankle.

N ame one of the circuses that visited Washington, D.C., before the Civil War. Find the answer on page 78 in the Did You Know? section and write it below.

,

___ ___ ___ ___ ___
 8   30

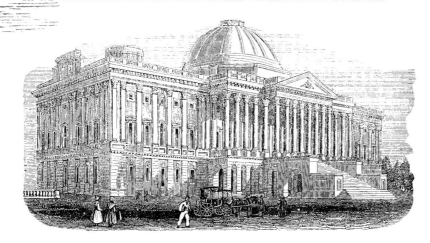

Capitol Building

George Washington laid the cornerstone of the U.S. Capitol building in 1793. Built of white marble and Virginia sandstone, it had a top that looked like a copper bowl. During the War of 1812, the British attacked Washington and burned the Capitol building. When it was repaired, plans were made to add a north and south wing and to replace the bowl top with a more stately iron dome. The work was finally completed after Lincoln urged it to be finished during the Civil War. He said, "If people see the Capitol going on, it is a sign we intend the Union shall go on."

A Union Camp

Going off to war to save the Union sounded exciting to young men in 1860. But the thrill wore off quickly! Boredom often filled the soldiers' day. Marching from battle to battle, they trudged through good and bad weather. They crossed mountains, rivers, and even swamps, often plagued by mosquitoes and forced to drink dirty water. Once they set up camp, the soldiers were given cheap food and little to do. Many got sick and died without even being in a battle. Yet despite the hardships, they kept up their courage by singing and writing letters to their families back home.

Uniform

Compared to the handsome uniforms of our armed forces today, the Union troops looked shabby. Each regiment wore a different uniform, and often these were mismatched, as men made do with what they could find. In time, Union forces settled on a blue uniform with various types of shirts and pants. A popular exception, even worn by Lincoln's older son, was a Zouave uniform. It had a brightly colored short jacket and baggy trousers and was originally worn by Napoleon's North African Army.

Oysters

Today oysters are considered a delicacy and served in expensive restaurants. But Northern soldiers would give them away if they had other food. This was because oysters didn't cost much during the Civil War and troops were served them all the time.

When Johnny Comes Marching Home Again

*Union soldiers and civilians sang this popular march-
ing song. Patrick Gilmore, the Union Army's leading
bandmaster, wrote "When Johnny Comes Marching
Home Again." But he did not use his real name.
Instead he wrote it as Father Louis Lambert.
Soldiers often made up added verses to popular songs
that told of their circumstances or were funny. See if
you can add another verse to these first two of
"When Johnny Comes Marching Home Again."*

*When Johnny comes marching home again,
Hurrah, hurrah!
We'll give him a hearty welcome then,
Hurrah, hurrah!
Then men will cheer, the boys will shout,
The ladies, they will all turn out,
And we'll all feel gay,
When Johnny comes marching home.*

African-American Soldiers

*President Lincoln said the courage
of the 180,000 black Union soldiers made victory possible. But
they were paid less, kept in separate regiments and commanded to
fight in the worst battles. And if
captured, whether former
slave or freeman, they were
treated as escaped slaves
and either killed or sold.
Yet in spite of all this,
they still volunteered to
fight and did so with
exceptional bravery!*

N ame a group of people who attacked
the president's stand on the war and
ending slavery? Find the answer on
page 35.

‾‾ ‾‾ ‾‾ ‾‾ ‾‾ ‾‾ ‾‾
14   10   9

‾‾ ‾‾ ‾‾ ‾‾ ‾‾ ‾‾
26   25   22

The Confederacy

Many Southerners had divided loyalties. They didn't want to leave the Union, but they didn't think the federal government had any right to meddle in their business. They wanted states' rights so they could keep slaves, which were necessary for their large cotton plantations. So they fought out of loyalty to the South and to save their way of life.

The Confederate flag (right) with a secession rosette and badge (below). The stars represented the seven original states that seceded from the Union.

President Lincoln promised a full pardon for all Southerners who renewed their allegiance to the United States. Look back on page 38 to find this pardon's name. It was called the Proclamation of Amnesty and . . .

___ ___ ___ ___ ___ ___ ___ ___ ___ ___
    27   28   3   12

President Jefferson Davis

Like President Lincoln, Jefferson Davis was born in Kentucky, but he grew up in a wealthy home and got a first-rate education. Later he became Mississippi's U.S. Senator and a spokesperson for the Southern states. He did not want war and worked to keep the South in the Union. But he was loyal to the South and withdrew from the Senate when Mississippi seceded. Shortly afterward, he accepted the Confederate presidency.

Currency

When the South started its new government, it needed money. So they printed some. But there wasn't enough gold to back up the paper dollars. As the Civil War continued, the bills lost their value. People started calling them "shinplasters" because they said the paper money was only good for bandages!

The Southern White House

As president of the Confederacy, Jefferson Davis moved to Richmond, Virginia. His home became the Southern White House. Today a museum of the Confederacy sits on its grounds.

Uniforms

Like the Northern troops, Southern regiments all wore different uniforms at first. But in time, they settled on a gray uniform. As the war continued, the South had no money to replace uniforms. So its troops wore faded and torn uniforms.

At the Battlefront

Soldiers from both the North and South fought hard during the Civil War. In battles at Shiloh, Bull Run, Gettysburg, Chickamauga, and others, they fought with cannons, rifles, and bayonets (knives attached to the ends of their rifles). Many were killed and wounded, but there was little medicine and few doctors. In the end, more Americans died in the Civil War than in both World Wars I and II!

A Civil War rifle with bayonet

Johnny Clem, the young drummer boy who joined the Union Army, fought in these battles. Look on page 38 of this book to find out their names.

— — — — — — — — — —
       7   1

— — — — —
   16

Cannon Balls & Canisters

This heavy iron ammunition had to be carried by two men. When supplies ran low, thin-walled canisters were filled with musket balls, sawdust, nails, hinges, and other scrap metal.

When these deadly rounds were fired from a cannon, the effect was like a giant shotgun. One soldier said, "It seemed as if whole companies were wiped out."

Lincoln at Antietam

President Lincoln visited the Union troops after they won the Battle of Antietam in September 1862. While there, he made his first announcement of the Emancipation Proclamation. He said that all slaves in the Confederacy would be free on January 1, 1863.

The dress hat of an artillery officer

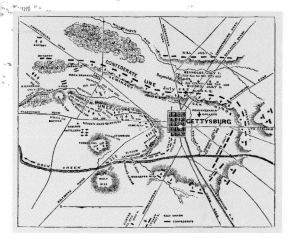

Confederate Commander Robert E. Lee

The Battle of Gettysburg

In June of 1863, Robert E. Lee, the confederate commander, marched his troops to Gettysburg, Pennsylvania, hoping for a major victory against the North. Instead he marched into the bloodiest battle of the war, in which 48,000 men died. He did not succeed and the tide of the war turned in favor of the North.

Swords and Scabbards

While soldiers fought with rifles and bayonets, officers often carried swords and pistols. Dress swords were popular off the battlefield and many had fancy, detailed hilts or hand grips. These swords were kept in cases called scabbards that were attached to a belt around the waist.

71

Behind the Lines

Today when our troops fight in a war, as much comfort as possible is provided behind the front lines. Doctors, medicines, and operating equipment help the wounded. Hot food is prepared regularly and entertainment is allowed as possible. However, in the Civil War this was not the case. Often supplies were scarce or en route, traveling slowly by wagon or railroad. Soldiers considered themselves lucky if they got three meals, hot or cold! And it was a bonus to have paper to write home on and a Bible to read.

Postage Stamp

After they seceded, the Confederate states scrambled to start a postal system. They chose the picture of Jefferson Davis for their first stamp. As the war continued, the popularity of letter writing caused these stamps to be more valuable than Confederate paper money.

Clara Barton

This "Angel of the Battlefield" earned her name by going to the front lines and walking among the wounded. Clara Barton could do little, but she offered water and bandaged wounds. When field hospitals and doctors were available, she assisted surgeons—even during shellings. This former teacher and patent clerk later founded the American Red Cross.

W ho was the first woman to receive her doctor's license? You will find the answer in the *Did You Know?* section on page 81.

___ — — — — — — — —
20

___ — — — — — — — —
23   2

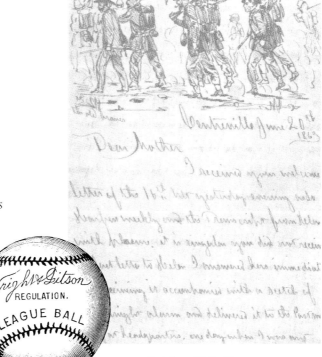

Field Hospital

Hospitals during the Civil War didn't have the standards of cleanliness our hospitals do today. Surgeons moved from one patient to the next without even washing their hands. Because of this, infection went unchecked and germs spread rapidly among patients. More soldiers died from illness than from fighting.

Baseball

Playing ball helped the soldiers cope with the boredom that plagued them between marches and battles. They took the game home with them after the war and played it with family and friends. In time, the rules stabilized and the ball game of the Civil War became the baseball we play today.

Medicines and Equipment

Although some organizations raised money for medicines and equipment, both the North and South often lacked even the basics. Brandy deadened pain and alcohol worked as an antiseptic, but often they ran out and nothing was available.

Soldiers Write Home

Civil War soldiers and their families kept the postmen busy. More letters were written during this war than any other time in our history. At times paper or pencils were scarce and often scraps of wrapping or envelope were used while one pencil would be shared by a regiment. Nothing cheered a soldier more than a letter from home.

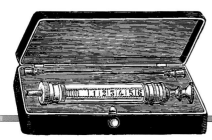

Union Headquarters

In a war lots of planning has to be done. Presidents and military leaders must decide where troops are needed, what is a good plan of attack, and how to defend their territory. They used information from spies and logical thinking to try and figure out what the Confederate generals would do. Sometimes their plans worked, but during the first few years of the war, they often did not!

Anaconda Plan

In 1861 Winfield Scott, general-in-chief of the Union Army, made a plan for the North to win the Civil War. The Union called it the Anaconda Plan—after a snake in South America that squeezes its victims to death. Scott planned to blockade Confederate ports and occupy the Mississippi river area—dividing the eastern and western Confederate states. If that failed to end the war, the North would invade the heart of the Confederacy.

The plan worked, but it took years—much longer than Scott expected.

Medal of Honor

To honor the many brave Union soldiers fighting in the war, President Lincoln signed legislation in 1861 that established a Medal of Honor. It was to be awarded to those who risked their lives "above and beyond the call of duty."

Today, this medal remains the highest military honor awarded by our country for bravery.

Observation Balloons

Without airplanes or radar, generals had to rely on runners to find out where troops were. To help with this problem, Professor Thaddeus Lowe, who owned three hot air balloons, used them to observe Southern military positions. It took 30 to 50 men to launch a balloon. Once the mooring line broke, and General Porter was almost carried behind Confederate lines.

The Draft

Early in the war more than enough volunteers signed up for both sides. As time wore on, however, and people heard about the death, disease, and lack of supplies, there were not enough volunteers. Both North and South gave cash awards to get men to enlist. In 1862 the Confederacy enacted a draft for men 18 to 35. The union followed with a draft in 1863.

W hat young man failed the entrance exam for West Point but went on to become a general anyway? You'll find the answer in the *Did You Know?* section on page 80.

___ ___ ___ ___ ___ ___   ___ ___ ___ ___
   11   15   5

The War Ends

Both the North and South suffered a great deal during the Civil War, and peace was welcomed by our battle-torn country. But the Union victory and Confederate surrender did not end all the problems the reunited Union faced. While Northern soldiers traveled home and went on with their lives, Southerners often had no homes to return to. Houses, farms, and whole towns were destroyed. Most had to begin all over again. President Lincoln wanted to help them, but as it turned out he was never able.

Slavery Ends

All slavery ended in the United States with the surrender of the Southern forces. Never again could one person buy or sell another.

Reverend Henry Highland Garnet (above), a former slave, became the first black man to ever speak before Congress, saying, "The blessings of peace are [now] equally enjoyed by all."

W ho made it rich off the South's misery? Find the answer back on page 39.

— — — — — — — — — — — —
 4   17 18   29

Go to page 82 to decode the message.

Surrender at Appomattox

Early in April 1865 General Grant stopped General Lee and his few troops from retreating out of Richmond. Lincoln only wanted the war to end, so he had instructed Grant to avoid all unnecessary bloodshed. Obeying the order, Grant sent Lee a note suggesting surrender. On April 9 the commanders met. Grant asked only that the army surrender and the men promise not to fight anymore against the United States. In a solemn ceremony the soldiers handed over their guns but were allowed to keep their horses.

Lincoln Shot Headlines

Shot while attending a play in Ford's Theater, President Lincoln was the Civil War's last victim. His death became the greatest loss since the birth of the nation. He was mourned not only in the North, but also in the South because the former Confederates knew Lincoln did not intend to punish them. John Wilkes Booth, Lincoln's assassin, thought he would be hailed as a hero in the South. Instead, newspapers across the North and South demanded his capture.

Ford's Theater

President Lincoln loved to laugh, and he planned to see Our American Cousin, a popular comedy playing at Ford's Theater. While enjoying the play from luxury boxes above the ground floor, he was shot by John Wilkes Booth. For years after the dreadful death of Lincoln, Ford's Theater remained closed, used only to store War Department records. But in recent years, it received its rightful place as a national historic site.

Reward Poster For Booth

In the days following the murder, reward posters for the arrest of Booth and his accomplices went up across the nation. Thousands of detectives, soldier,s and ordinary people entered the search. And in the end, Booth was caught and shot when he refused to leave a burning barn where he was hiding.

Henry Clay

Black Hawk War

This four-month war began when a Sauk Indian chief named Black Hawk tried to reclaim his tribe's land on the east side of the Mississippi River. When settlers panicked and shot at the Indians, a short war started that ended in Black Hawk and his band being pushed back across the river.

Battle of Gettysburg

Fought in northern Virginia, this three-day battle helped the North win the Civil War. But it cost our country a lot. By the time it ended, more than six thousand soldiers were dead, thirty-two thousand were wounded, and ten thousand had been taken prisoners.

Circuses

Circuses have traveled throughout the United States, entertaining folks since the early 1800s. A couple of circuses that came to Washington, D.C., before the Civil War were the Great Southern Circus and Welch's National Circus.

Henry Clay

This American statesman was called "the Great Pacificator" because he resolved problems that threatened to tear our young country apart by thinking of compromises. Though popular in Washington, men like Abraham Lincoln stood against his slavery compromises. He lost presidential elections three times. He died in 1852, and his funeral is recorded in Frank French's journal.

East Capitol Street

The street where our fictional heroine lived is the same street that Frank French lived on. Later the French home was torn down and the present-day Library of Congress building was constructed on that location.

Did you

A Circus Clown

Ford's Theater

The theater where John Wilkes Booth performed as an actor as well as where he shot President Lincoln is at 500 10th Street NW, only a few blocks from the White House. People can still visit it today.

Francis O. French

Raised in Washington, D.C., "Frank" lived from 1837 to 1893. He kept a journal for two years when he was twelve through fourteen years old. He lived at 37 East Capitol Street with his parents, Benjamin and Elizabeth French. He attended Mr. Wright's Rittenhouse Academy and later Phillips Exeter Academy and Harvard. Though he was admitted to the bar, he became successful in banking rather than in law.

The Stonewall Jackson, a Confederate River Defense Ram

Ford's Theater

Everything You Ever Wanted to Know about the Time of Abraham Lincoln

know?

Godey's Lady's Book

This magazine was started by Louis Godey in 1830; seven years later, Sarah Hale became its editor after her husband died and she was left with five children to support. Under her leadership it became the largest magazine for women in the United States. For thirty years it influenced American women. But after the Civil War, American society changed, and its popularity declined. It continued until 1877, when Sarah Hale retired at ninety years old.

Letters

Americans wrote more letters during the Civil War than at any other time in our history—more than even today when the population is several times larger! Though ink and paper became scarce and mail service undependable, soldiers and their families still managed to correspond. Toward the end of the war, Southern postage stamps were more valuable than Confederate money.

Lincoln's Invention

Abraham Lincoln is the only United States president who took out a patent for an invention. On May 22, 1849, Lincoln took out U.S. Patent No. 6,469 for a lift to take boats over underwater sandbars.

John Wilkes Booth

Lincoln Memorial

Thirty-six columns hold up the porch of this memorial, which is built like a Greek temple. It has three rooms: one has the large marble statue of Lincoln; another contains the Gettysburg Address; the third has his second inaugural speech in it.

Mexican War

In 1846 President James Polk wanted California, then held by Mexico, to become a part of the United States. He claimed a battle between American and Mexican soldiers north of the Rio Grande made it necessary to declare war on Mexico. Congress voted in favor of this war, but many objected to it, including Abraham Lincoln.

Thomas (Tad) Lincoln

Lincoln's Sons
Abraham and Mary Lincoln had four sons: Robert, Edward, William, and Thomas. Robert served in the Civil War. Edward died of consumption when he was only four years old. Willie's birth comforted his parents after the loss of Eddy, but when his father was president he died of either typhoid or malaria. Thomas or Tad Lincoln was born with a cleft palate that was surgically repaired.

Turkey Buzzard

Mrs. Howard's Academy
Mrs. Howard was one of many educators who established private schools in Washington, D.C,. in the early 1800s. Common subjects taught included reading, writing, sewing, painting, music, dance, and French. Many public and religious schools also existed in our capital city during the 1800s.

Murder Trial
William "Duff" Armstrong was defended by Lincoln against the charge of murdering another man. Armstrong's mother, Hannah, asked Lincoln to defend her son, swearing that no son of hers could kill a man in a brawl. Lincoln won his release by using an almanac.

New Salem
The town that young Lincoln moved to after leaving his family only survived a few years. Built on the Sagamon River in 1829, its residents hoped that steamboats would come up the river and turn it into a boomtown. But by 1840 people gave up on the town and abandoned it.

Omnibus
These first buses were pulled by horses. The driver sat above and outside the bus with a rope tied to his leg. When someone wanted off the bus, they pulled on the rope. Young boys standing by the door collected the riders' fares until collection boxes were later hung from the ceilings.

Pucker
This nineteenth-century term referred to someone being irritated or angry.

Republican Party
In the years before the Civil War, our country had two major political parties, the Democrats and the Whigs. But as the issue of slavery spread to new territories, folks got riled up and the big parties split apart, creating new antislavery parties. One of these parties sprung up in Ripon, Wisconsin; members called themselves Republicans. They wanted a strong central government, high trade fees, and other policies the South didn't like.

School Lessons
Paper and pens or pencils were not usually used for school lessons. Instead, students had workbooks or small slates or boards and chalk. Though Lincoln frequently had to use boards to write on, he did use some workbooks that have been preserved at the Columbia University Library, the Chicago Historical Society, the Library of Congress, and in Brown University.

General William T. Sherman

William Sherman
Second only to Ulysses Grant, this Union general fought in battles

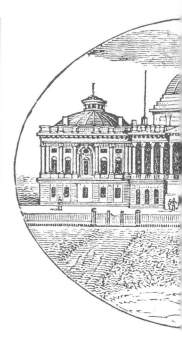

such as Shiloh and Vicksburg. Often called the "first modern general," he destroyed crops, railroads, and anything else that would cut off supplies to the Confederate Army. He is best remembered for his "March to the Sea" through Georgia and South Carolina, where he left a path of destruction. Soon afterward, the South surrendered.

Johnny Shiloh
This young hero of the Civil War was discharged from the Union Army right before the end of the war. President Grant appointed him to West Point, but he failed the entrance exam several times. Finally, Grant made him a second lieutenant. He went on to become a brigadier general.

The U.S. Capitol

Smithsonian Castle

This sandstone palace looks like a castle out of King Arthur's day. Its towers and turrets were finished in 1855 thanks to James Smithson, an Englishman who gave half a million dollars to build it. Today the "castle" is part of the Smithsonian Institution, which houses a huge selection of American artifacts and has been called "the Nation's Attic."

Stonewall Jackson

This Southern general got his nickname because, though outnumbered, he couldn't be budged by the Union Army at the first Battle of Bull Run. In clash after clash, he proved to be a great military leader. He won many famous Civil War battles such as Fredericksburg and Bull Run. However, in the Battle of Chancellorsville he was accidentally shot by one of his own troops. He died a week later, two years before the war ended in a Union victory.

Turkey Buzzard

The bird that Abraham Lincoln took quills from to make a pen is the largest vulture in North America. It lives off dead and dying animals and has wingspans of up to ten feet. It's red-skinned bald head and hooked beak make it hard to miss.

War Medications

At the time of the Civil War, antibiotics, pain relievers, and other lifesaving drugs had not been developed. Therefore, wounded soldiers were mainly treated with alcohol, usually in the form of whiskey or brandy. A medicine known as "blue mass" also was popular. It supposedly cured everything from toothache to digestive problems. Quinine, known to relieve malaria symptoms, was also used for many other illnesses.

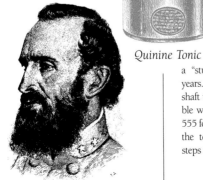

General "Stonewall" Jackson

Quinine Tonic

Walt Whitman's Poem

O Captain! my Captain!
our fearful trip is done,
The ship has weathered every rack,
the prize we sought is won,
The port is near, the bells I hear,
the people all exulting.
Exult, O shores, and ring, O bells!
But I with mournful tread,
Walk the deck my Captain lies,
Fallen cold and dead.

Washington, D.C.

When our country was first formed, Congress met in Philadelphia until a capital city could be built. Three commissioners chose the location of present-day Washington, D.C., and it was named after our first president. George Washington picked a French engineer to plan the city, but it didn't get built fast. When the government officially transferred to the city in 1800, shanties and swamps surrounded the unfinished Capitol building and the president's house.

Washington Monument

This memorial to our first president remained a "stump" for more than twenty years. Finally, in 1884, the hollow shaft with outer walls of white marble was finished. It stands just over 555 feet with an observation room at the top. An elevator or 898 iron steps take a person to the top room.

Walt Whitman

White House

Known as the President's House for many years, this elaborate residence was the center of social activity during the mid-1800s. Unlike today, people had easy access to the president, and often they came seeking jobs and favors. In his diary, Frank French describes visiting the president three times, including once to get his autograph.

Women's Rights

Sarah Hale believed in women's rights but was careful to always present her ideas in a ladylike way. Her ideas were far ahead of her time as she advocated that women should get exercise and medical training. Sarah helped organize the first women's college, Vassar. She also lived to see the first American woman get her doctor's license—Elizabeth Blackwell.

BECOME A NEWSPAPER

Correspondent

Now that you've completed the activities, be sure that each blank below is filled in with the appropriate letter from the previous pages. When all are completed, you will know the headlines that appeared in the *Jamestown Journal* announcing the end of the Civil War.

——— —— —— —— ——   ——— —— —— —— —— —— —— ——
 1   2   3   4   5   6   7   8   9   10 11 12 13

——— —— ——   —— —— —— —— —— —— —— —— ——   —— —— ——
14 15 16   17 18 19 20 21 22 23 24 25 26   27 28 29 30

Congratulations! You're an official My American Journey newspaper correspondent!

Lincoln and Slavery
Lincoln stood against slavery, saying, "If the Negro is a man, why then my ancient faith teaches me that 'all men are created equal,' and that there can be no moral right in one man's making a slave of another."

Final Answer: Glory! Richmond and Petersburg Ours!
5-Chickamauga and Shiloh, 6-Elizabeth Blackwell, 7-Johnny Shiloh, 8-Carpetbaggers
Answers to clues: 1-Turkey Buzzard, 2-Welsch's, 3-Armchair Generals, 4-Reconstruction,